Spring Snowman
Adapted by Jill Barnes
Story and Illustrations by Fusako Ishinabe

GEC **GARRETT EDUCATIONAL CORPORATION**

A snowman stood all alone,
high on a mountain.
The children who had built him
did not come back to play.

Everything was cold and quiet.
It was winter.

One day the snowman heard
animals running along.
They were on their way
down the mountain.

"Why?" wondered the snowman.

The animals stopped
to wave to the snowman.

"Where are you going?"
he asked.

"Down the mountain," the bear said.
"Spring is coming!"

"Spring?" the snowman said. "What is that?"

The squirrel said, "Spring is warm. It is not
cold like winter."

"Spring is wonderful!"
the white rabbit said.

The animals waved good-bye
to the snowman.

They went running down
the mountain, and he
was left alone again.

The snowman was sad.
"What's wrong with winter?"
he wondered.
"And what is spring?"

Days went by, and the snowman
still stood in the forest.

The sun shone longer every day.
The snowman felt strange.
Something was happening to him.

Down at the bottom
of the mountain,
the snow was melting.

The cold days of winter
were over.

16

The white rabbit ran off by herself.
All around her she saw the beautiful
pink cherry blossoms.

It was really spring!

When the grass was green
and the sun was warm,
the animals started home.

They stopped to pick flowers to take
to the snowman.
They planned to tell him about spring.

But when the animals came
to the place where the snowman
had stood, he was gone.

A little melting snow was all they saw.

It was sad, but spring is not
a time for snowmen.

The animals went on, but they
looked back and waved as if
the snowman could see them.

One day the white rabbit began
to point to something she had found.
"What is it?" the bear asked.

"A surprise!" the rabbit said.

The white rabbit showed the way.
The animals hurried as fast
as they could.

29

What they saw made them stop.

Where the snowman had stood
in winter, white flowers bloomed
in the sunshine.

Could it be a spring snowman?

Maybe it was!

Edited by Caroline Rubin

U.S.A. text copyright© 1990
by Garrett Educational Corporation

SPRING SNOWMAN by Fusako Ishinabe,
Copyright© 1983 by Fusako Ishinabe
Originally published in 1983 in Japanese,
under the title "HARU NO YUKIDARUMA"
by KAISEI-SHA PUBLISHING CO., LTD.,
English translation rights arranged with
KAISEI-SHA PUBLISHING CO., LTD.,
through Japan Foreign-Rights Centre

Manufactured in the United States of America

Library of Congress Cataloging-in-Publication Data
Barnes, Jill.
Spring snowman/adapted by Jill Barnes:
story and illustrations by Fusako Ishinabe.

    p.   cm.

    Summary: A snowman is curious about spring,
when flowers bloom and the animals play.
ISBN 0-944483-83-6
[1. Snowmen - Fiction. 2. Spring - Fiction. 3. Animals
- Fiction.]
I. Ishinabe, Fusako. Haru no yukidaruma.
II. Title
PZ7.B2623Sp 1990   90-37748
[E] - dc20   CIP
                               AC